For Josephine Pagan with love   RS

To Jay, for all your help and encouragement —
this one's for you   TW

Text copyright © 1995 Ragnhild Scamell
Illustrations copyright © 1995 Tim Warnes

First published in Great Britain in 1995 by ABC

This edition first published in 1995 by softbooks,
an imprint of ABC, All Books for Children,
a division of The All Children's Company Ltd,
33 Museum Street, London WC1A 1LD

Printed and bound in Singapore

British Library Cataloguing in Publication Data
Scamell, Ragnhild
Who Likes Wolfie?. — New ed
I. Title II. Warnes, Tim
823.914

ISBN 1-85704-073-2

Who Likes Wolfie?

Story by Ragnhild Scamell
Pictures by Tim Warnes

softbacks

"No one likes me," said Wolfie.
"Of course they do," said his
friend Bird, from the safety
of a tree.
"Who?" asked Wolfie.
Bird thought for a moment.
"Well, there's...um...and..."

"You can't think of anyone,
can you?" said Wolfie sadly.
"No one likes me."

Bird felt sorry for his friend, but it
wasn't really surprising that no one
liked Wolfie. He wasn't very nice.
"I like you," said Bird firmly.
"And I'd like you even better if
you smiled a bit more."
Wolfie looked up and gave Bird
a big smile. "Like this, you
mean?" he beamed.

Bird almost slipped off
his branch when he saw
Wolfie's sharp, white
teeth. He tried not to,
but he just had to jump
on to a higher branch.

"No, perhaps it's better if you don't smile," said Bird. "What about doing something that is really, really nice?"
"I can sing," said Wolfie. "Is singing really, really nice?"
"Yes," said Bird. "I'm very good at singing, myself."

That night, as the moon began to rise over the snowy slopes, Wolfie marched with his brothers and sisters to the top of the highest hill. He stretched his neck towards the moon.

"Auoohuu," he howled,
just to test his voice.
"Aaoohuu," echoed his brothers
and sisters.
A herd of reindeer that had been resting
nearby scampered away.

Wolfie checked that Bird
was sitting in his tree. Then he
took a deep breath, craned his neck as
far as it would go towards the big, silvery
moon, and began to sing:

It's so hard to be good when you're bad
Oh, I'm bad and it's making me sad
It's so hard to be good
Though you know that you should
Oh it's hard to be good when you're bad.

"A-a-ad, Auoohuu," harmonized his brothers and sisters.

"Stop that racket!" shouted Polar Bear from his cave. "There are bears here, trying to sleep!"

But Wolfie didn't hear him. He was spellbound by the round, silvery moon and he just had to sing.

I'll be glad when I'm no longer bad
When I'm good I shall really be glad
It's so hard to be good
Though you know that you should
Oh it's hard to be good when you're bad.

"Baahaahad-Aaoohuuoou," harmonized his brothers and sisters.

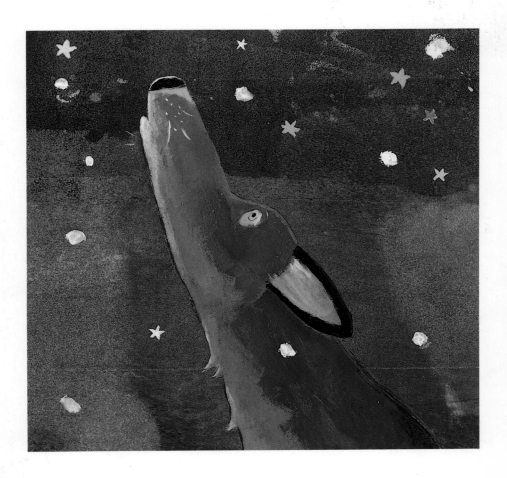

When the final note had
been sung, Wolfie turned
and smiled at Bird, who was
still sitting in the tree. His big,
sharp, white teeth glistened
in the light from the
silvery moon.

"Right," said Bird. "Yes, very um . . . nice."
"Really, really nice?" asked Wolfie.
"Not bad," said Bird.
"I'll do it again, if you like!" said Wolfie.
"No, no," protested Bird.
But Wolfie did it again and, as he sang, a
warm feeling of happiness spread through him.

Polar Bear and his family, the
herd of reindeer, and quite a
few rabbits had gathered
around Wolfie and his brothers
and sisters. They looked tired
and angry.

"I think they're getting to like
me," Wolfie winked at Bird.

Bird didn't know what to say.

Just then, a beautiful shadowy creature
appeared from the woods. Wolfie saw her,
as he always saw anything that moved.
His heart beat faster, and he howled his
song to the moon with such feeling that
Bird had to bury his head under his wing.
   "Auoohuuoou!"

Never had Wolfie seen anyone as beautiful as she. As she walked up the snowy slopes, her coat sparkled in the moonlight. Her eyes shone with a yellow light and her razor-sharp, white teeth glistened so perfectly that he was afraid her soft pink tongue would be hurt.

Polar Bear, the reindeer and the
rabbits stood aside. They, too, had
seen those sharp, white teeth.
    She didn't stop until she was right
beside Wolfie. She smiled at him and
his chest swelled with pride.
    "That was really nice," she said.
    "Really, really nice?" asked Wolfie.

"Really, really nice," she said.
"Just like you!"

For a moment, Wolfie was so happy
that he couldn't speak.
   "This is a verse just for you," he told her.
   And, as he stretched his long neck
towards the moon, Wolfie knew that
someone liked him.

I just know that I'm no longer bad
It's so nice that I've stopped being sad
It's a joy to be good
I just knew that I could
It's not hard to be good when you're bad!